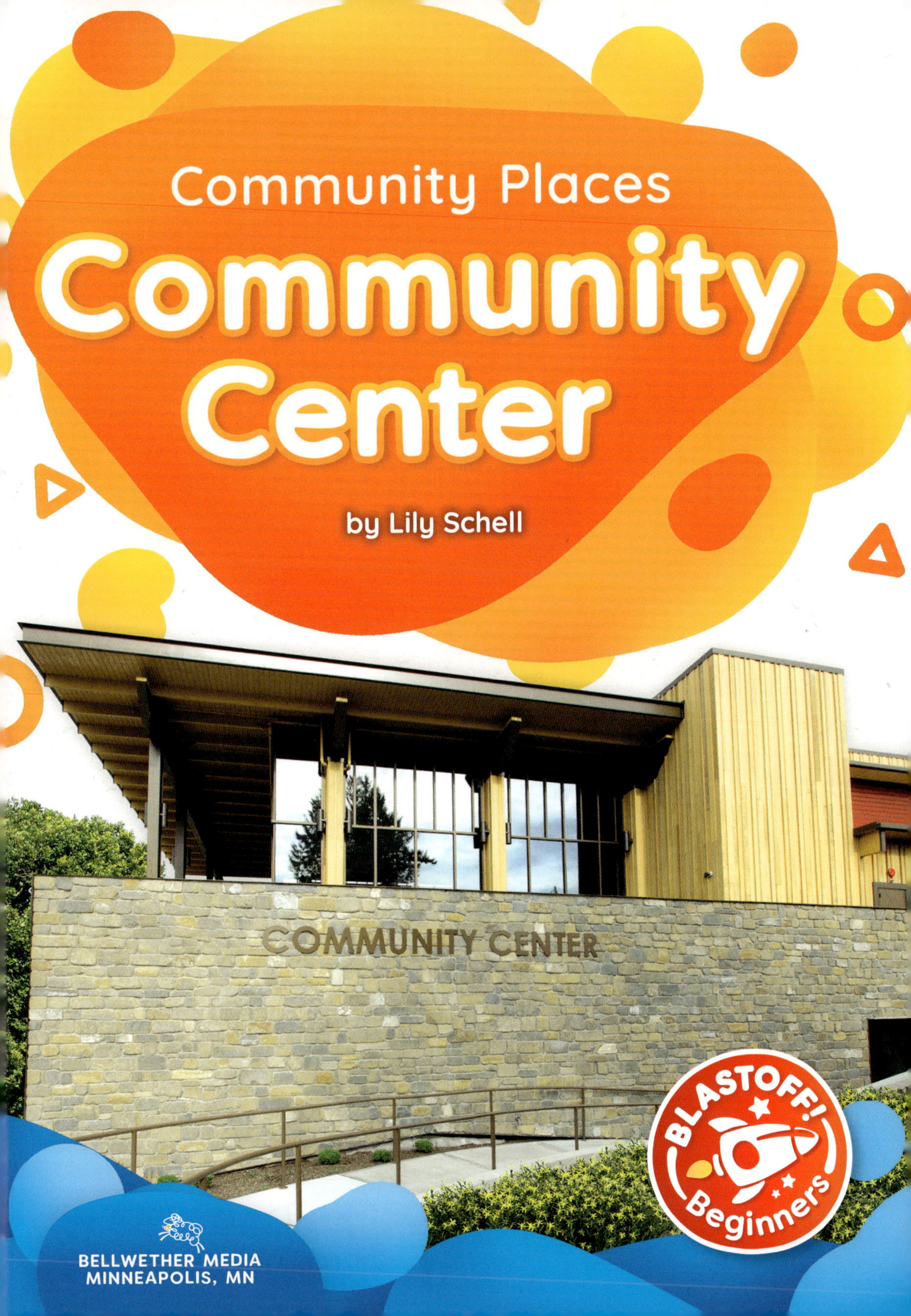

Community Places
Community Center
by Lily Schell
COMMUNITY CENTER
BLASTOFF! Beginners
BELLWETHER MEDIA
MINNEAPOLIS, MN

Blastoff! Beginners are developed by literacy experts and educators to meet the needs of early readers. These engaging informational texts support young children as they begin reading about their world. Through simple language and high frequency words paired with crisp, colorful photos, Blastoff! Beginners launch young readers into the universe of independent reading.

Sight Words in This Book

a	go	run	use
about	have	the	we
are	make	them	will
at	out	they	you
can	people	to	
do	play	too	

This edition first published in 2023 by Bellwether Media, Inc.

Library of Congress Cataloging-in-Publication Data

LC record for Community Center available at: https://lccn.loc.gov/2022002370

Editor: Betsy Rathburn Designer: Gabriel Hilger

Printed in the United States of America, North Mankato, MN.

Table of Contents

At the Community Center!

We will learn
to swim.
We are at the
community center!

What Are Community Centers?

Community centers are **public** buildings. They have a lot to do!

Success
Starts Now!

Towns run them.
Cities run them, too!

OCEAN CITY
COMMUNITY CENTER
Aquatic & Fitness Center · Art Center · Public Library · Historical Museum · Senior Center

So Much to Do!

Kids go
after school.
They stay safe.
They have fun!

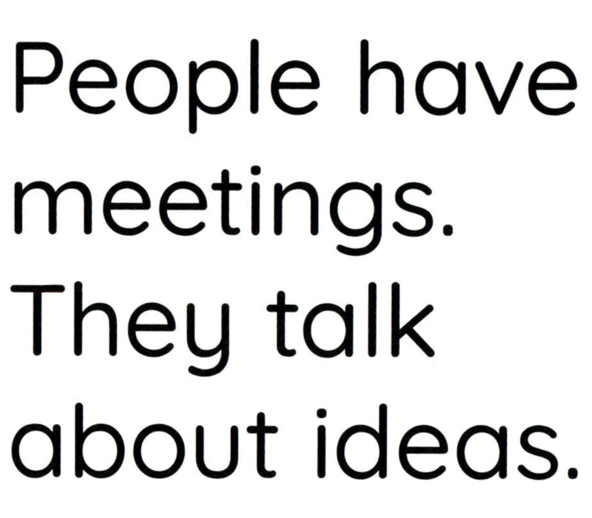

People have meetings. They talk about ideas.

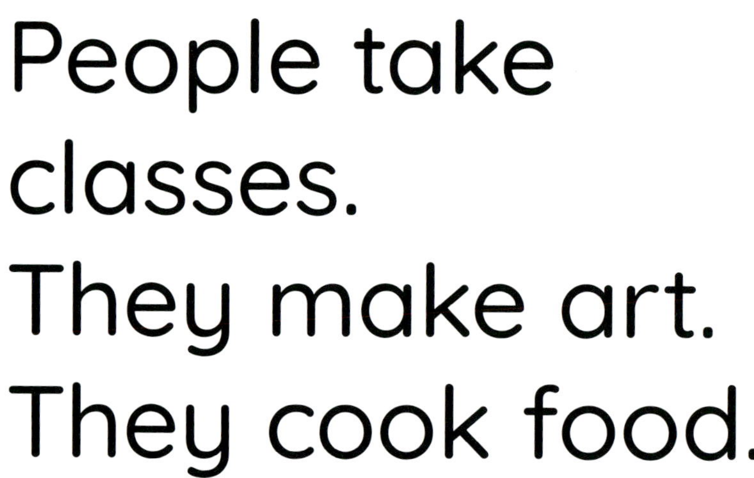

People take classes.
They make art.
They cook food.

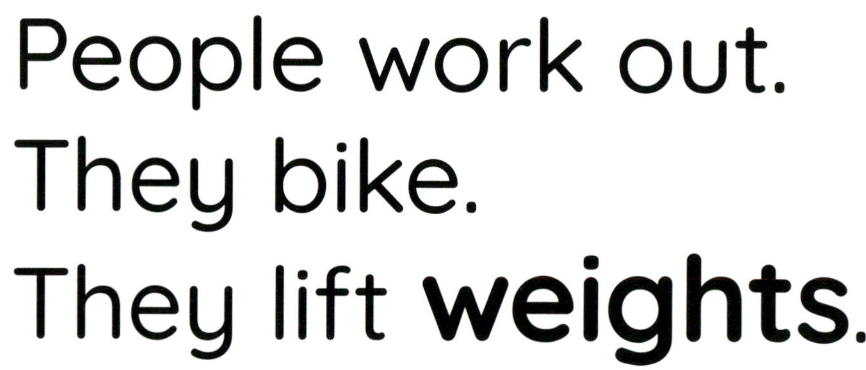

People work out.
They bike.
They lift **weights**.

Kids play basketball. They use the gym.

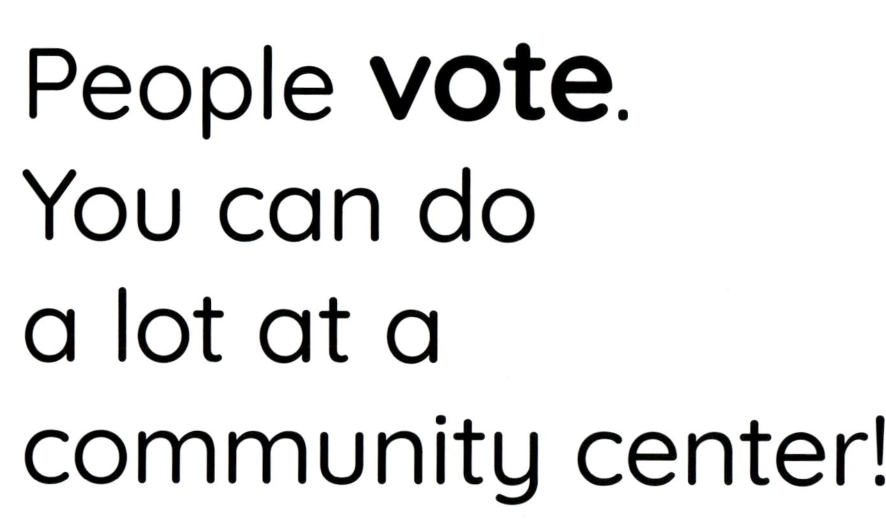

People **vote**.
You can do
a lot at a
community center!

VOTE
VOT

Community Center Facts

At the Community Center

What Happens at a Community Center?

learn to swim

have meetings

take classes

Glossary

open to everyone

to choose leaders and give thoughts on changes to laws

heavy objects people use to get stronger

To Learn More

ON THE WEB

Factsurfer.com gives you a safe, fun way to find more information.

1. Go to www.factsurfer.com.
2. Enter "community center" into the search box and click 🔍.
3. Select your book cover to see a list of related content.

Index

The images in this book are reproduced through the courtesy of: njpPhoto, front cover; Luis Louro, p. 3; Nataliya Turpitko, p. 4; Monkey Business Images, pp. 4-5, 12-13, 14-15, 22 (have meetings); Jose Luis Pelaez Inc/ Getty Images, pp. 6-7; Rosemarie Mosteller, pp. 8-9; FatCamera, p. 10; GagliardiPhotography, pp. 10-11; Jeffrey Isaac Greenberg 7+/ Alamy, p. 14; dencg, p. 16; Wavebreakmedia, pp. 16-17; Dmytro Zinkevych, pp. 18-19; vesperstock, pp. 20-21, 23 (vote); Muk Photo, p. 22 (at the community center); Microgen, p. 22 (learn to swim); Pressmaster, p. 22 (take classes); Rawpixel, p. 23 (public); wideonet, p. 23 (weights).